FIFO 2

How a Drug Dealer became a FIFO worker...

Aaron Weston

www.facebook.com/aaronwestonauthor

www.instagram.com/aaronwestonauthor

www.tiktok.com@theaaronwhiteshow

DEDICATION

I dedicate this book to my wonderful family and to all the fantastic FIFO workers and their families. I hope that you enjoy the book.

DISCLAIMER

This book is a work of fiction. All characters and events in this book are fictitious and any resemblance to real persons, living or dead is purely coincidental.

ISBN-13: 978-0648701118

Johnno

Hi guys, let me introduce myself and give you a heads up on what you are in for. I'm Johnno and this is my story of how I went from being your friendly neighbourhood drug dealer and user to... yes, yes, I know, I was breaking the number 1 rule of the drug game, you never get high off your own supply. Anyway, as I was saying, from drug dealer and user to FIFO worker and maybe I find love along the way.

This is not your average book; it is a wild ride with a no holds barred writing style. You will think OMG, I cannot believe the author wrote that and the funny thing is, he is just writing what you or your best mate are thinking. The only thing is, he is not afraid to say it. This is because he really does not mind if he offends you. It is your choice if you get offended or not. Ask yourself, "Do I really need to be offended by what someone else says or does, or can I just roll my eyes and walk away?"

Boom! Going deep already and it is only the first couple of pages. Ha ha.

But, if you do get offended, just do what us miners say and go down to your local Bunnings and have yourself a spoonful of concrete and harden up. Ha ha, seriously though, thanks for buying the book, you are supporting your local Australian author pay off his rehab fees. Hey what can I say? I had to do research to get into the head of each character.

Grab yourself something to eat and a drink, so you do not have to get up. Now click in your seat belt, as you prepare yourself for a hilarious and confronting movie that is about to start playing in your head. That is what an awesome book does, you start picturing what you are reading and even make up what the characters look like. Boom! Another great statement. Wow! This book is on fire, and it has only just begun. Ha ha.

I think I will start with this story.

I have seen other dealers at nightclubs try to pass off a Ritalin pill as an Ecstasy pill, hoping the customer does not look at the pill and just pops it straight into their mouth in a hurry, as not to been seen purchasing illegal drugs by a security guard or an undercover cop. I am sure it works a lot of the time and Wow! What a profit margin. If that dealer has a script, which means he can purchase a bottle of 30 pills at $38.30 that is $1.30 each and then sells it at a club for $50 that's $48.70 profit, times that by however many pills he sells that night. Boom! He just made more in one night than someone would earn all week doing a 9 to 5 and it is all tax free.

One night, I did see it backfire on Sam, one of the other local dealers. He was smartish as he had real Ecstasy pills and the Ritalin pills in his pockets. He would sell real Ecstasy pills to the older, more seasoned party goers, knowing they would check the pills and if they liked them, tell their mates to go and see him to buy some. Also, they would check the pills just so they could see what logo was on the pills. There are many different types of Ecstasy pills and to tell them apart, each make of pill have their own logo pressed into them. Some have a dove picture pressed into the pill or a car make, like a Mitsubishi symbol. Some of the party goers like to brag after the night or weekend is over about what a killer time they had, they would say things like "Dude, I was so fucked up. I had 3 white doves and 2 green Mitsubishis, and I was off my head. Bring on next weekend."

I watched Sam one night as he did the Ritalin / Ecstasy trick to a young 18 year old, who looked as if it was his first-time buying drugs. As the kid gave Sam the $50 in exchange for the pill. The kid turned around and started to walk towards a group of older guys probably in their mid-20's that Sam had not realised the kid was with, and who would definitely know what's what with the pill. Thinking quick Tim called out to the kid.

"Oi, undercover cop. Quick, swallow it."

The kid looked stunned but instead of chucking the pill into his mouth he shoved it deep into his pocket and ran over to the group. One of the guys who I am guessing is the kids' older brother was watching the whole thing and asked the kid for the pill. I could see the blood draining from Sam's face, if that were me, I would have just turned and walked away. That being said, I would never have sold the fake pill in the first place, as I am a big believer in karma, and I do not rip people off as I do not want to be ripped off myself.

It was interesting watching Sam and the older brother. The older brother looked at the pill, realising his brother had just been ripped off, looked at Sam and Sam was looking at him, but Sam did not move, he was frozen, and I guess that is why they say there are three responses to danger; fight, freeze or flight.

The brother and his four mates went straight for Sam. Sam jumped to life and started through the crowd. Unfortunately for Sam it was a busy Saturday night, and the club was packed. It did not take long for the group to surround Sam and push him into the toilets. I felt like helping Sam, but I am a lover not a fighter and the couple of mates I did have there that night were busy cracking onto girls.

So, all I could do was wait for the guys to come out of the toilets, which they did after about 5 minutes. They were all laughing, and the older brother was handing out stuff to his mates. I would take a guess that he was handing out the rest of Sam's gear, that they had just stolen off him. Like I said karma. Once the coast was clear I made my way into the toilets.

There were a couple of guys peeing in the piss trough pointing and talking about something that was in one of the stalls. I walked over and pushed the stall door open. Sam was laying there on the pee covered floor in a heap, crying.

"Hey Sam, are you alright?" I asked.

He turned to look at me. Wow! Those guys really did a number on his face. His left eye was already swollen, he had a fat lip that reminded me of a Kardashian and a bloody nose with blood covered snot pouring out of it, down his mouth and onto chin. Yuk!

"They beat me up and stole my money and gear," he replied and then he blew out a big pile of the bloody snot into his two hands and wiped it onto his jeans. Double Yuk!

I had already guessed as much, karma. But it would not of helped the situation by telling him that.

"Can you get George for me?" he asked.

"George? Who is George?" I replied.

"He's the big Maori security guard out in the club."

"Umm, alright," I replied, and I pulled a big handful of toilet paper from the roll and half handed, half dropped it into his hands. Come on, I did not want to get any of his snot or blood on me.

I headed out of the toilets and back through the crowd in search of a big Maori security guard. The crowd was going off, they were dancing with glow sticks, drinking and cracking onto each other. Oblivious to what had just happened in the toilets. I make my way up to the bar and look around. There he is, a big Maori security guard, gee whiz he is towering over the crowd. I wonder if he is standing on a platform or a ledge. I squeeze back through the crowd to reach this guy and as I get up to him, I realise he is not standing up on anything, he is just a beast. I tap on his shoulder, and he leans down to me.

"What's up Bro?"

"Are you George?"

"Yep."

"Sam told me to come and get you. He's been bashed and mugged."

"Oh, for fucks sake, I'm sick of this shit. Where is he?"

"He's in the toilets," I replied while pointing to the toilets.

"Alright follow me."

I followed behind this grizzly bear of a bloke as he steam-rolled his way through the crowd. He was like a bowling ball knocking pins over. A couple of guys turned around ready for a fight but one look at George they quickly changed their mind and turned back around and avoided eye contact.

We arrived at the toilets and George pushed through the door almost taking it off its hinges. A guy who was in there washing his hands turned his head in surprise. He took one look at George and decided to quickly exit the area.

George pushed open the stall door and looked down at Sam, who was still crying, and his face was covered in dried blood and snot.

"For fucks sake Sam, did you try to rip off someone with those fake Ecstasy pills again?"

"Maybe? They took my money and the rest of my gear."

"I'm Fucken over this Shit. After I get your stuff back, we are done. Do you hear me? I'm getting grey hairs from this Crap."

"There were five of them."

"Great," he turned and looked at me. "Did you see these guys?"

I nodded.

"Alright, come and point them out."

I did not want to get involved in this any further. But at the same time, I did not feel comfortable saying no to George. We went back onto the dance floor to look for the guys. I spot the guys at the bar doing shots, I am guessing it was Sam's shout.

"There they are, those five at the bar doing shots."

"Good, come on."

Off I go following him like a little bitch, too afraid to say, "Sorry mate, this is not my problem," and just walk off.

"You lot, come with us," George said sternly in his security guard tone.

"What? Why? We haven't done anything."

"Yeah. Why are we getting kicked out?"

George just led them over to a side door which led out to a back exit.

"This is bullshit. We haven't done anything."

"Whatever, this is a crap club anyway. Let's go to the Mustang Bar."

"You guys aren't going anywhere."

The guys looked at each other with shocked and confused expressions of their faces.

"Give me the stuff you stole off Sam. Now!"

"What? We don't know what you're talking about," said the older brother who was obviously the alpha of the group. George stepped closer to him and wrapped one of his bear paws around the guy's neck and started to squeeze. The guy was hitting and wrestling with George's hand, to no avail and he was starting to pass out. My eyes were drawn to the guy's crotch, and I could see it was becoming wet and it was getting wetter and wetter. The poor bloke was pissing himself.

"Here, here. Let him go. Just let him go."

They all started pulling out the drugs and money that they had taken from Sam and pleaded with him to take it, shoving it into his free hand. George dropped the guy onto the ground.

"I'll take the rest," he said while looking down at the older brother. The friends quickly went through his pockets and pulled out the rest of the gear and money.

"Here, can we just go."

George waved them away. These guys were no heroes, they were just a group of mates out for a good time, and I feel if Sam had not tried to rip them off, they would still be enjoying their night and they were not out looking for victims to mug. They probably just got caught up in the moment and caved into either peer pressure or the pack mentally, or I could be totally wrong, and they were just a pack of dickheads.

Anyway, off I went with George back to the toilets to fetch Sam. When we got there Sam was up at the sink washing the blood and snot off his face.

"Good, you're up. Make sure you wash all that crap off. I don't want any getting on my seats," George said.

With that, Sam dried his face with paper towel, and we followed George through the crowd. It was like watching Moses' part the Red Sea. Actually, I think I will stick with the bowling bowl through the pin's analogy. Ha ha.

We hop into George's car, it is a F250 which is quite spacious. I guess being George's size, he would have to have a big car, or else it would be too uncomfortable.

We drive for about 20 minutes and end up in a nice, respectable, older suburb.

"Is this your place Sam?" I asked as we pulled up to a nice older house.

"Yeah, well actually it's my Grandma's."

"Oh, okay," I say, sounding surprised.

"Yeah, well after my parents split up, I decided I didn't want to live with either of them. They were just so negative, and Grandma said I could move into hers."

"Fair enough."

We went inside and it was your standard grandma house, family photos on the wall and a wooden Jesus Christ nailed to a cross thing up on the wall. I wonder if she knows what Sam does for a living.

"Sam is that you?" came the voice of an elderly lady.

"Yes Grandma. I have George and a mate with me too."

We walk into the kitchen and there was an elderly lady, probably in her mid to late seventies doing a jigsaw puzzle.

"Hi George," she said smiling and kind of giving off a flirtatious vibe. Ha ha, good on her, still flirting at her age. He would probably break her in two or give her a heart attack if he were to have sex with her. Yuk! Why did I picture that? Double Yuk!

"Hi Judith, how are you going? Having a win?"

"I have all the outside pieces done. Do you want to join me?"

"Maybe next time."

"God Samson, look at your face. George are you not supposed to be looking after him? Is that not what we pay you for?"

"Sorry Judith, he ripped off some guys by selling them Ritalin instead of Ecstasy again."

"Well, that's karma Samson. What have I always told you? If you treat your customers right, they will always come back. A man is only as good as his reputation."

"Yes Grandma."

Judith turned her attention to me.

"Sorry Hun, how rude of me for not introducing myself. Normally a man would introduce himself to a lady, but I understand equal rights and all that," and then she paused, giving me a look as to say, "Well are you going to introduce yourself?"

"Oh, sorry. I'm John."

"Nice to meet you, Johnathon."

"No, just John. That's what's on my birth certificate."

"Well, nice to meet you, John. I am Judith. So how do you know these two?"

"Johnno is a drug dealer too, Grandma."

"Well, if you need any supplies just let us know. I am sure we can get you a better price or at least better-quality gear," Judith said to me.

"What? Really. How did you get involved in this?" I blurted out, not thinking before speaking.

Sorry to make it awkward. I was just taken off guard. When did Betty White from The Golden Girls start selling drugs?

George gave me a look to say "Shut up" but it was too late. It is funny how a look can say so much. I guess that is why they say a picture tells a thousand words.

"Tea or coffee?" Judith asked everyone.

"Coffee please," we all replied. Really? What kind of person our age drinks tea? Unless you are a Pom, I guess.

"Well Johnathon," Judith started.

"John," I corrected her.

George rolled his eyes.

"Yes, sorry John. Well, when my Henry went to be with the lord, five years ago. He did not leave me with much, besides a mortgage. I thought we were debt free and had savings. You see with my generation; the man was in control of the finances and the lady runs the house. It was not my place to ask about the finances, I wish I had. I was left to rely on the pension, and I soon realised that the pension is next to nothing. I was about to sell my home just so I could pay the bills. But God was looking out for me and at that same time my daughter Jeanette and her husband Cedric decided to separate, and Jeanette asked me if I would like Samson to live with me and do the upkeep around the house. Truthfully, he is not very handy when it comes to fixing things around the house. But he gave me an opportunity to get out of financial trouble, keep the house and now I even have saving of my own and I can afford a cruise or a couple of nice outings each year."

"Yeah, when I realised how financially messed up Grandma was, I asked her if she would like to turn her spare room into a hydro set up and she has always liked gardening so voila, she grows it and I sell it. She even has some of the ladies from her lawn bowls club growing some for us too. The pension is shit and no one is going to employ a seventy to eighty year old, not when they can employ a twenty to forty year old for the same price. They would be too worried that they would fall over and break a hip or something and claim worker's comp."

"Thank you, Samson, you are right. It is a lot harder for people of my age to get employment and there is nothing wrong with marijuana. It will be legalised one day or at least decriminalised once the people in charge wake up to themselves."

"Fair enough," I replied.

We hung out for a bit and drunk our coffees.

"Come on Johnno, I'm cruising. I can drop you off home on the way," George said to me.

"Yeah, cool."

We hopped back into his small truck, and I told him my address.

"Why are you dealing drugs Johnno?" he asked.

"It's easy money and I wasn't particularly good at school. I was never going to be a doctor or anything special."

"Ever thought about going up north to the mines?"

"Na, not really. Why's that?"

"Well, I'm sick of this security crap and having to deal with idiots. So, I am going to hit my cousin up for a job. He is a supervisor up at a mine just out of Port Hedland. I can ask him for a job for you too if you want?"

"Yeah, why not? I'm up for something different."

"Cool. Here is your place and I'll be in touch."

We pulled up in front of mine and swapped phone numbers. I did not expect him to call. I am used to people talking shit. I have learnt to just smile and agree.

A week or so later, I was down at the Left Bank in East Fremantle having some fish and chips, when my phone started vibrating. I looked down and saw the caller ID was George.

"Hello."

"Hey bro, it's me, George. How are you going?"

"Yeah, good thanks. How are you?"

"Yeah, sweet as. Hey, I got you a job if you're still keen."

"Oh shit. Umm. Well yeah cool. Ah. Wow! You kind of put me in a spot. I thought you were talking shit."

"Na bro, I don't talk shit. Well, I am heading up on Thursday, next week. You can either come with or not. Up to you?"

"Umm, yeah. Can I think about it?"

"Can do, I guess. Give me a call back."

"Yeah, will do and thanks for actually doing what you said you were going to do. I'm just not used to it."

"No worries bro. Hit me back when you are ready."

And with that he hung up. I sat there for a while watching the cars and trucks go over the traffic bridge and did some soul searching. I cannot just drop everything and go up North. I have responsibilities. What? No, you don't. Yeah, what am saying no I don't. There is no reason I cannot just drop everything and try FIFO out for a bit. Exactly. Why am I answering myself? Maybe I just need someone to agree with me that I am doing the right thing and there is no one else here to do that but myself. Sounds about right. Ha ha, I am stopping that right now and I am calling George back before I can back out.

"Hey George."

"Gee, that was quick, but I guess all the girls say that to you. Ha ha."

"Nice one. Anyway, I'm in. What do I have to do?"

"Cool. You will have to do a drug test. Wait, do you think you would pass one?"

"Yeah, the stuff I take only stays in your system for a couple of days and I haven't had anything for... must be around 4 to 5 days now."

"Good, I'll email you the chick from the recruitment agencies details and just get in touch with her and she'll sort you out. Let me know how you go, and I'll pick you up on Thursday, next week, if it's all good."

"Awesome, thanks again."

"Yeah, no worries. See you."

He hung up. Wow! And just like that, I guess I am giving up the drug game and picking up the FIFO game. It is funny, my dad always told me I should get a trade or a degree, you know, something to fall back on. I just could not do four years on apprentice wages or, four years at university, where I would have to pay them for it, just so that I can get an eighty grand a year job and due to George, I will probably be on a hundred grand a year straight away. Yeah Buddy!

Two days later, I went in to do my drug test and it was so weird. I did not realise a guy had to literally stand there looking at my dick while I take a piss. I guess there must be a lot of pot smokers who try to use someone else's urine to pass. I have heard of a fake penis being used and I did not give it too much thought, but now it all makes sense, he would see the fake penis and the fake urine coming out and think it is yours.

Anyway, I had massive stage fright and it took ages and about two litres of water to finally do a pee. And thanks to that I was pissing every twenty minutes for the next three hours.

Wow! What a job, having to look at guys dicks all day. I guess if you are gay, you would probably be in heaven. I probably should not say that, as it is not politically correct and apparently just because you like the same sex you are not attracted to every guy, or girl if you are a lesbian, but whatever, this book is written to contain some shock value and political incorrectness. It worked for Eminem, so will all the real Slim Shady's please stand up, please stand up.

I passed the drug test and I told George. He told me the job he got me will be on the blast crew, blowing shit up. Sounds totally badass.

Thursday morning came along, and I was all organised for it, the night before. I had packed my bags and set my alarm for 3.30am so I would have plenty of time for a coffee and a shower to wake me up, as George was picking me up at 5am.

Bang, Bang, Bang.

"What the hell was that?" I woke up startled.

Bang, Bang, Bang.

"Who is it?"

"George, who else would it be?"

"Shit, my alarm didn't go off."

"Well, we have to go. So, you have 5 minutes or I'm going without you".

"Okay, okay."

So much for my shower and coffee, but luckily, I had packed my bag last night. So, I chucked on some clothes, grabbed my bag and jumped into George's car. God, I felt yuk, I always have a shower to wake myself up.

"Alright, let's do this," I say.

"You look half asleep. Why didn't you wake up earlier and have a shower and a coffee?"

"Ha ha. Yeah well, that would have been a great idea."

We both laughed and head off. We went through a Macca's on the way, and I got myself a coffee and something to eat.

I will fast forward the airport stuff, as this book is supposed to be read after FIFO number 1 and I do not want to bore you by repeating the same stuff too much.

I did make the mistake of getting a seat next to George. The gorilla took up his seat and half of mine.

"Move over. You're pushing me through the window," I say.

"How about I put you in the overhead compartment? Ha ha."

"Whatever, I'm moving."

"Sorry Sir, you will have to take your assigned seat during take-off and landing. When the fasten seat belt sign is turned off, you will be free to walk around the cabin or sit in another seat," the cute airhostess said.

"Great, thanks."

I had a great view on take-off and landing, thanks to my face being squashed against the window. Trust me, I will not be making that mistake again.

George and I finally made it to the mining camp, and we were greeted in the office by a fat chick with too much make up on.

"Hi, are you two checking in? I haven't had the pleasure," she purred.

I burst out laughing. I did not know if she was serious or joking. Sorry, I know I am no Brad Pitt but come on, I can do a lot better than this chick. I must give it to her though, she had some confidence.

"Whatever. Anyway," she replied to my laughing. Now focusing all her attention on George. "My name is Shirley, and I will be assigning your rooms."

I started to wish I had not laughed. I bet I will now get a crap room. We gave Shirley our names and she tapped away on her computer.

"Here is your room, P12 and here is a map. I am sure you'll find it easily enough," she said to me, while handing me a map and the key, at the same time keeping her eyes locked on George like a tiger would its prey. "And as for you, your room is a bit harder to find. So, I will take you there. Follow me," she said while licking her lips at George.

I burst out laughing again, while leaving the office. I could not help it; it was the funniest thing I had seen in ages. It was like a bad romantic comedy; it was so obvious she was gagging for it. I wonder if George would have sex with her. He is not a bad looking bloke and could do a lot better than her. I am not gay or nothing, but you know if a guy is ugly or not. Off I went to find my room using this photocopied treasure map. Not a bad looking place, it looks like a holiday camp that you would find at Uluru, you know Ayers Rock or somewhere like that. There was even a couple of kangaroos hopping around which added to the whole nature aspect. I grew up in Fremantle and we never did much camping. We did stay in Dwellingup for two nights for a school camp once, but that was about it. So, this whole bush thing is a bit of a novelty. It was bloody hot though. I guess I will have to get used to the heat if I am going to be working out in it and I am sure I will climatise after three weeks up here. George landed a dump truck job, so at least he will be in the air conditioning.

I found my room and chucked on the hi-vis clothes the recruitment agency gave me and the steel cap boots that they told me I had to buy.

Knock knock. I spun around and saw a short bald guy in his early forty's. He kind of looked like Carl Barron, the stand-up comedian.

"Hi, are you John?"

"Yep."

"I'm Pete, your supervisor. Once you are ready, I'll take you to site and show you around."

"Okay, cheers."

Pete and I cruised around the Pit, which is just a massive hole in the ground. I saw the drill rigs, they look like something out of Star Wars and the dump trucks are massive, they are about the same size of a town house. Pete handed me over to Steve, the blast crew leading hand.

"You'll be with Steve for the rest of today. Then over the next two days you will be doing inductions," Pete says before driving off.

"Alright Johnno, I'll give you the two minute pitch on what we do. We spray paint dots onto the ground, in a three meter by three meter grid pattern. Then the drillers come in and drill a hole where the dot is, down to a certain depth. We lower a tape measure down the hole to make sure it is the correct depth, if it is not, we get the drill back in to re-drill it. Once all the holes are good, we lower a booster and a detonator down each hole. Picture a stick of dynamite with a string tied to it. Next, we fill the holes halfway with ANFO, which is just Amino Nitrate and Diesel. Then we fill the rest of the hole with loose blue metal. Lastly, we connect all the detonators together and blow up the ground. Boom! Done. Ha ha. That is what we do. Then the diggers and trucks come in and remove the dirt and we start all over again. Pretty easy."

"Sounds easy enough, I guess."

I spent the next year or so doing that and selling drugs on my breaks, just to my mates. There was no reason to take any unnecessary risks like selling to a random, who might end up being an undercover cop and getting your stuff confiscated. Before, I did not really care because I did not really have anything worth confiscating but today is different. Today I picked up my dream car a

HSV Commodore. God, it is so sexy and shiny, it is black with sick mags and a big 5.7 litre engine and to top it off, I have a hot date with a couple of chicks that I met off the internet. I hope when they see this beast of a car, they get all excited. I am excited just to drive it. I never expected to drive, let alone own a car of this calibre. Ha ha, and my teachers told me I would never amount to anything. Now I earn more than they do, and my ride would definitely be a lot nicer than theirs. They could only wish they had a ride like mine.

Maybe I should do a couple of laps slowly past the school just in case one of them is outside and see me. Then I would wave to them, and they would be like "Oh my god, was that Johnno who I used to teach, gee I was so wrong about him. He is doing so much better than I gave him credit for. Wow! What am I doing with my life?" Then I would laugh and drive away leaving them in their self-pity. Ha ha. More than likely, they would just call the cops saying some guy is acting weird slowly driving past the school like a creep. Umm, on second thoughts I will just do some laps of the main street, it is called the cappuccino strip here in Fremantle that is because on either side of the road are the coffee shops and cafes. All the guys and girls drive their cool cars up and down it. So yeah, I will do that so everyone can go "Wow! Check out that cool ride." Wow! I feel like such a tosser saying this but honestly this car does make you feel cool. See classic example, check out that guy over there staring at me and my ride, wishing he were me. Look how excited he is and envious. WTF, now he is even waving, he is a bit too keen, a bit desperate.

"Hey Johnno, what the hell? Are you a drug dealer or something?" the guy asked.

It took me a sec; I know his face from somewhere. Oh, that's right he is that guy from school that fell off the sheep. Mich, Mike, no Mick. That's it, Mick.

"Ha ha. Na mate, I got myself a job in the mines doing FIFO. I'm on the blast crew."

"Okay, so what is FIFO? and what is the blast crew?"

WTF, this guy lives in WA and does not know what FIFO is. It is only one of the biggest industries in WA.

"FIFO means you have to fly into the middle of nowhere for three or so weeks, then fly home and have a week off and you come back cashed up. The blast crew blows the ground up, and then the earth moving machines come in and dig it up."

"That sounds good. Any chance you can get me a job doing that?"

"I probably could. I will ask my supervisor and see what he says."

"That would be awesome. Thanks Johnno."

We exchanged phone numbers.

"Hey, I have to go. I am meeting up with a couple of chicks I met off the internet. I hope that when they see me driving this beast, their panties will fall off, ha ha."

"Alright, have fun."

With that I cranked up my stereo, ACDC just happened to be playing on the radio and I put my foot down to show off how fast the car can go. The tyres started spinning and I accidently did a burn out and almost lost control of the car and came centimetres off hitting the curb. God, pull your head in mate, you do not want to crash your pride and joy, on the first day you bought it.

Anyway, I cruise over to pick up the chicks. Driving a bit more cautiously mind you. I will have to get used to the power before I try showing off again, which is bound to happen a lot. Yeah, this beast has a lot more power than my old AU Falcon.

I pull up to the address the chicks gave me, and I rev the engine to show off the car and to announce I have arrived. I guess that is fine as I am safely parked, in neutral and park brake applied, ha ha.

"Oi, Dickhead. Stop revving your engine like a Tool," yelled out a try hard looking bikie guy.

That comment snapped me back to reality. Maybe I was driving around today in a bit of a fantasy, and I did not look as cool as what I thought, and I was actually acting like a Tool.

"If you are here to pick up my Charlene, get out of the car and knock on the door like a gentleman. Not like some prick who thinks he is the man and guess what? You are not. You know what they say about guys with big cars? Little dicks."

Wow! Definitely a wakeup call. Back in the day I would have been intimidated by this kind of guy. But he is just some want to be bikie. I work with real patched members at work, and they will smash this try hard if he lays a finger on me.

Just as I was thinking this, two patched members walk out of the front door. Shit, maybe this guy is not a want to be, and he is a real bikie. So, I turn off my car and walk up to the front door where they are now all standing staring at me trying to intimate me. Honestly, it is working but I cannot show them that. It is like with a horse, as soon as you show you fear it; it will buck you off. Or so, I have heard. I have never ridden a horse.

"Hi, I am Johnno and sorry about that. New car and I am still getting used to it. Is Charlene ready?"

The guys just stood there staring at me. Wow! What a group of dickheads, big dickheads that could smash me, and just to think, I thought I was the only one acting like a tosser today, but these three are up there with me.

"For fucks sake Dad. Cut it out."

A bogan chick with tattoos and piercings burst out from behind the three guys.

"Come on Johnno, let's go. Shit, hot car. Can I drive? Actually, better not, I am pretty half cut, and I cannot afford to get another DUI."

She walked, well really ran over to the passenger side of the car. I do not think it is just alcohol she has been taking.

"Come on, let's go and have some fun," she yelled back at me super-fast. Yep, she has had a couple too many lines of speed or God knows what.

Anyway, I did not need to spend any more time standing on the front lawn with these idiots. I jumped in the driver's seat and chucked on my seat belt.

"Wow! You are hot," she said.

"Thanks, you too," I replied. Starting to feel better about myself. Got to love a compliment.

"Let's go pick up Trace. I'll show you where to go."

She cranked my stereo to full volume almost blowing the speakers and my ear drums.

"See ya, losers. Ha ha," she yelled out the window.

We pulled up at a Home's West / Housing Commission looking house with overgrown lawn and kids toys and bikes in the front yard. Charlene leant over me and pushed down the horn. Beeeeeep!

"Oi slut, come on. Let's go," she screamed through me and my open window. If I was not deaf from the music, I was now. Thanks Charlene. Charlene? What a bogan name. I wonder if there is a book with all the bogan names in it and the bogan parents read it and say that sounds trashy and you know what? I might even spell it incorrectly and I will just blame it on my poor education or the fact that I was drunk when the missus popped out the kid. Anyway, Crystal with a K, Krystal sounds good, or Kandy I am quite sure that is how you really spell it. Kotton Kandy sounds good because she will be sweet like Kotton Kandy or more realistically she will be full of sugar from the crap diet we are going to feed her. Oh snap, did I just drop a real-life truth bomb?

Quick Language Warning. If you get offended by a couple of skanks talking as they do, please skip the next few pages. But if you do, you may miss out on some funny stuff.

Out of the front door came a tattooed, pierced up skinny chick breast feeding a baby. WTF.

"Oi slut, I'll just be a minute. I just gotta finish feeding Axel."

She went back inside and three minutes later came back, baby less.

"Fuck Mum, I told you I will be back tonight. No, I don't know what time. You'll be right you had six of us," she yelled back inside the house.

Yeah, and probably to six different dads all paying child support, what a career she has, professional mum. That being said, the dads are probably not paying child support, they are probably in jail or drug addicts. Wow! Judgemental much.

The funny thing is, I am the one that is attracted to these damaged girls. What does that say about me? I simply better pull out or use a condom because I do not want to be on a list of baby daddy's working up north and paying child support. There is enough of them in the mining industry already.

"Oi slut, you look hot," Charlene said to Trace.

"You too, and you look hot too mate. Wanna get a girl pregnant?" Trace asked me and both girls burst out laughing. I laughed too just so it was not awkward. That was probably the worst pick up line I have ever heard, at least I will get one in tonight. I looked at Trace's breasts and I could see wet patches on her shirt over her nipples. She looked down.

"Oh shit, the taps didn't turn off. Don't worry I'll be back."

And off she went, as if it was no big deal.

"You want to do a line?" Charlene asked, while at the same time grabbing one of my cd cases and racking up 3 perfectly straight lines.

"Yeah, why not?"

How funny is life? Here I am doing lines of speed in front of a Home's West house in a car probably worth more than the house, while waiting for the chick who lives there to turn off her breasts. How much stranger can this day get? Ha ha.

"Normally, I would shoot this up. You know because it's a cleaner way to do it. Straight into the blood stream, not having to stuff around in your nose or stomach and possibly wasting some of it. But I ran out of needles last night and it probably does not look the best, bringing a needle on the first date. You might think I am a junkie or something. Ha ha."

And it just got stranger. Ha ha.

"Ha ha. I don't judge," I said just before snorting up my line. Whoop Whoop! Yeah Buddy! That is some good stuff right there. That is not cut with anything, straight from the lab. Damn. Those bikies always get the good stuff. Probably because it comes straight from the manufacturer and is not cut with Epson salts or God knows what.

"Oi, you better have one of those for me," Trace said as she approached the car with a new top on. Her tits looked massive compared to her small frame. You could see a little bit of a gut pushing against her top or would you call it loose skin? I guess that is bound to happen when you pop out a kid.

"Can you have drugs when you are breast feeding?" I asked surprised.

"Yeah, why not? My Mum did with us, and we turned out fine. All that stuff in the news is full of it," she replied while hopping into the back seat and grabbing a rolled-up note from Charlene to do her line.

"Fair enough," I say. I do not think there is any point trying to argue about not taking drugs when you are breast feeding with this chick. As my mother always said, there is no point arguing with a stupid person. Stupid is as stupid does. (All said in my head, in a Forrest Gump accent)

"Your shout Johnno, let's swing past the bottlo."

"No worries," I say, as I put my foot down. The speed had kicked in and I was in GO mode. I looked at the speedo and I was doing ninety-five in a fifty zone, better zone down, I do not want to get my car impounded on the first day.

We swing through the bottle shop, and I order a carton of vodka cruisers. Well, try to order, Charlene keeps cranking my stereo and the girls are yelling to each other to talk over the blasting music. I had to repeat myself four times to the bottle shop guy, before he could understand what I wanted. He looked pretty envious. I guess I cannot blame him, he had to work and here I am driving around this flash car with two chicks in it. Good times.

We cruised around Fremantle and up to Scarborough following the coast. It is a nice drive, up through all the rich areas surrounded by mansions and other nice cars. I saw a Ferrari drive past and thought of that scene in Fast and Furious when they had just finished doing up the orange Toyota Supra and they pull up on that Ferrari and smoke it.

"Oi Johnno, I'm horny let's go back to yours."

Enough said, and I do an illegal U-turn right there at the traffic lights. I guess that is why I like this kind of girl, no games, they just say what they want. As if I want to take a girl on fifty billion dates, just to get to first base, when all I must do is get them pissed and they are ready to go.

Do not worry, I am not going to go too X-Rated. Just in case you are a bit prudish. But then again, I guess you would have stopped reading this book if you were, so here we go.

As I go to turn into my driveway, Charlene grabs my crotch. It surprises me and I turn early and Bang! I drive straight into my letter box.

"Fuck."

I reverse back and drive up my driveway correctly and jump out of the car.

"Shit, fuck, fuck."

I had scratched up the front fender of my car, luckily, it was not bent. I could probably get some touch up paint or something. Still annoying as though.

"Don't worry about it Johnno. Focus on us," Charlene says while winking at me. I change my focus and focus on the present. It will probably be better sex now, as I now have a bit of resentment towards her for causing me to scratch up my car. What did I say? You know what I mean. Why do you think the sex is better after an agreement? It is because of the resentment and blame. I hope you know what I mean, otherwise maybe it is just me and I have some issues to work out. Maybe I was not hugged enough when I was young. Hmm.

Anyway, back to the present.

"Yeah, all good. Come inside," I say while forcing a smile and opening the front door.

"That's what she said. Get it, come inside her. Ha ha," Trace laughed.

Ha ha, it was a good one. That made me have a genuine smile. I love the old, that's what she said lines. That being said, I do not think I will be coming inside her; she looks like she would get pregnant at a drop of a hat or a drop of semen.

We settle in and crank up the tunes. Charlene pulls out her speed and we do a couple of lines each. I relax on the couch drinking a Wild Turkey and coke, watching the girls do a sexy strip. This is the life, what could go wrong? What an awesome day.

I look at Trace's full breasts, I must admit they look good on her small figure but then I see the wetness on her nipples, not much, but I start thinking of her nipples with the milk as big pimples and it is turning me off a bit. I know breast milk is natural and this is what breasts are made for and I am sure this would probably be a turn on for a lot of guys, but yeah na, not me. I change my view and concentrate on Charlene; she is hot as.

"Get those pants off and come here Johnno," Charlene demanded.

Yes ma'am, and I rip off my jeans and shirt, so we are all naked.

"Why aren't you hard?" she asked.

Damn it, whipper dick. If you have not heard of this reader, let me educate you. On drugs, some guys can get hard and go for hours and find it hard to cum. But other guys like myself just cannot get it hard and I have even had days when it has shrivelled up and looked tiny like a micro penis, I was on other drugs at the time, so I do not know exactly which drug caused it. That being said, when I am sobber and get it hard, it is a good size. Do not be thinking I am just some small dick bloke who cannot get it up.

"You got whipper dick?" she asked.

I guess she has seen this before. I start playing with it to get it hard, it is not working.

"You know my dad's mates can get it up for ages and it's great."

Wow! That is going to work, demeaning me by comparing me to your dad's mates and picturing you getting gang banged by them at some club house. Good one.

"I'll be back," I say and walk off into the bathroom. When I am in there, I start pulling at it, splashing water on it, flicking it back and forth. I am getting a bit more volume but no hardness. I hear spinning wheels and a big burn out going up the street. I am not too surprised there are plenty of bogans on my street. I walk back into the living room and the girls are gone and so are my keys.

I pull the front door open and see a big set of skid marks leading up the street. Fuck. I start running after my car and I hear a loud wolf whistle. It is one of my neighbours, I look down and I see I am completely naked. WTF. I spin back around and sprint even faster back into my house. What was I thinking? As if I could have caught them on foot. I put some clothes on and try to think of my options. Should I call the cops? No look, there are drugs on the table and what if they search my house? I have drugs stashed in the house and I am pretty pissed too. Would they even believe me? Who can help? I know I will call George. Yep, that is what I will do. I find my phone, at least they did not steal that as well.

"What's up bro?" George answered.

"They stole my fucken car."

"Who stole your car?"

"Two crack whores."

"Ha ha ha ha ha ha. What? Ha ha. Sorry I should not laugh but what the fuck?"

"I met two chicks off the internet, they got me drunk and high, and stole my car when I could not get my dick hard."

"Ha ha. That is so crazy. So, two chicks tried to date rape you, but you could not get it up, so they stole your car instead. Are you messing with me?"

"No, I'm serious. Can you help?"

"Just call the cops."

"I can't, I'm high and they might not believe me. You did not believe me. Can you come over?"

"Alright, alright. I will be over in twenty."

"Twenty? That's ages."

"God, have a shower and clean yourself up. I am sure you probably look as good as you sound. Don't worry you have insurance. You have insurance, right?"

"Yes, I have insurance. The dealership made sure I had it before I left the yard."

"Alright, see you soon," he hung up.

I hid the drugs and cleaned up a bit just in case we do call the cops and I had a quick shower to make myself look presentable.

Bang, bang, bang.

"Yo, Johnno, open up."

"Glad you're here."

I told him everything that had happened.

"Well, get in my car and we will go for a drive and see if we can find your car. Hopefully, they just went for a joy ride and have not wrapped it around a tree and killed themselves," he said.

My mind was racing. What if they have crashed my car and killed themselves? Is that my fault? I guess it would be, if I had never hit Charlene up on the net, then we would never have caught up and she would still be banging her dad's mates and Trace would be breast feeding one of her hundred kids. This is all my fault.

"Shut up Johnno. We will find your car," George said.

Wow! I thought that I was thinking that and not talking out loud. Am I talking out loud now or thinking it? I got to get off the drugs I am going crazy. Please God do not let the girls be dead. I am not a Christian by any means, but I will pray. God if you can hear me, please let my car be safe and the girls be safe and alive. If you do that for me, I promise I will give up the drugs for good.

"Is that your car?" George said pointing to my HSV parked across 3 parking bays at the Mosman Park beach car park.

"Yep, it is. They must be swimming."

George pulled up alongside my car. The doors were wide open, and the keys were still in the ignition.

"Straighten your car up. Otherwise, if the cops drive by, they might think something is up."

I straighten up my car. I felt like driving off and just leaving the girls. How dare they steal my car. But I did pray to God, so I do kind of have to check to see that they have not drowned in the water.

We locked our cars and headed down to the beach. They were easy to spot, all we had to do was follow the trail of scattered clothes on the beach into the water. There they were catching waves completely naked.

"Not bad looking birds Johnno and you could not get it up, WTF."

"Yeah, and na, like I said too much speed."

"Maybe I'll see if they want some of this? and I think I will hide my car keys before I do them. So, I do not wake up with no car. Ha ha."

"Ha ha. Good idea."

"Oi Johnno, come for a swim and bring your mate," Charlene yelled out from the water.

"I'm keen. Let's go," said George.

"Yeah, why not? Maybe the cold water will wake my dick up."

We both strip off and run into the water. God the water is fresh, and it feels great. Oh yeah, that deal with God, yeah well, a deal is a deal. I will give up the drugs. What is the point of being on them if I cannot get it up anyway?

"You are a big boy, aren't you?" Trace said to George.

"Ha ha. Thanks for noticing and it gets bigger. Ha ha."

We swam around for a while, catching waves and George was flirting up a storm with Trace. I was also having fun with Charlene; she is actually, a really cool chick. Also, I could feel some movement coming from downstairs.

"You guys want to come back to mine and chill?" I asked everyone.

"Yeah, I'm getting hungry I might do a Macca's run first. Trace, do you want to come with me?" George asked.

"Hell yeah, let's go," Trace replied.

Those two dried off and took George's car for their Macca's run. While we dried off and hopped into mine. I was waiting for a sorry I stole your car, but it never came. She probably did not think it was a big deal. So, I decided just to let it go otherwise it would just ruin the day and what is the point of holding onto things.

"You want Macca's or something else?" I asked Charlene.

"I feel, Asian."

"Well, you don't look Asian. Ha ha."

I know, that was such a dad joke.

"What about Wok in a Box?" I ask.

"Yep, sounds good. I could go some chicken Pad Thai."

"What? That is my favourite. I always get that one."

"Yeah, it's the best."

We drive off and get our chicken Pad Thai's. Buzz Buzz. I look down at my phone and there is a message from George.

"Trace and I are heading to mine. See you at work (wink face emoji)."

"Wear a condom," I write back.

Hey bros before hoes. I do not want George accidently becoming baby daddy number five and be stuck paying child support for the next eighteen years.

We get back to mine and chill watching Vikings on Netflix, eating our Wok in a Box. We chat through the whole first episode. She told me she wanted to be a vet while she was growing up, but her dad just put university down and schooling in general, saying it was a waste of time. He never went past year ten and could not understand why she would want to be in school any longer than she had to. Basically, he just did not understand her and all he wanted her to do was to hook up with one of the members in his club and become someone's old lady. Then the guy would provide everything she needed, and she could just hang out and have fun. Then eventually pop out a couple of kids. I told her all about me and being on the blast crew and how hopefully one day I will be on the drills. It is a lot more money and you get to sit on your arse all day in the air conditioning. Sounds a lot better than working out in the heat with the flies.

We cuddled up for a bit to watch the next episode. It was nice and comfortable, especially as it was just us two, no Trace and George, or her dad and his mates. We had not done any more drugs since she had stolen my car, so my dick was firing on all cylinders. We had sex and then cuddled up in bed and she spent the night.

We spent the next couple of breaks together and we both changed our Facebook status to "In a relationship" which felt cool. It is only official when it is Facebook official. Ha ha.

I am back at work and 2 weeks into my swing, and you know what time that is? It is shift change time. Which is always fun, straight after work we all hit the wet mess (the pub) and get on the piss. I normally bring up some speed for the boys, to make a bit extra cash and Pete brings up some Ecstasy. Do not worry, I kept my deal with God, and I am not getting high off my own supply.

I told Charlene about the deal I had made with God, and she thought it was the sweetest thing ever. She told me she has never had anyone pray for her to be alive and to give up drugs in exchange for the chance that she is alive. In her world that would be unheard of. Due to that, she promised to stay off the gear too. We were even talking about getting gym memberships, but we have not done that yet, one step at a time.

Ha ha, look over there, it is Shirley on the prowl and yep, she has got Mick in her sights. He had come straight out of the toilets and walked into the sightlines of the huntress. The lioness is sizing up her pray, she is about to pounce on her unexpecting victim. Still unaware, the pray walks straight into the pathway of the lioness, she licks her lips and what is this? She is playing with her food. The pray looks around for help, because he is new here, help is hard to find, Boom! He locks eyes with one of the only people that can save him. Yes, it is me Super Johnno ready to save poor victims from the camp bike. His eyes are full of fear and pleading for help, "Save me, I am about to get sexually harassed." Sorry buddy no HR here. But alright I will save you. I flick my head to say come over here and that, is his out. He says his excuse for leaving the lioness's claws and runs to safety. Ha ha, it is like watching a nature documentary.

"Ha ha, I see you have met Shirley," I say.

"Yeah, I thought she was going to eat me."

"Yeah well, she will if you let her. She has done heaps of the guys around here and the wet mess on shift change is her hunting ground. Ha ha."

"What, no way. Who would have sex with her?"

"You would be surprised. There are many lonely, horny guys up here and add a lot of alcohol and voila some poor sucker is waking up next to a grizzly bear. Ha ha. Hey, do you want to do a line?"

"What? You mean drugs?"

"Umm, yeah. What else? I bring up some speed for shift change every swing and Pete over there brings up the Ecstasy."

"Really, how do you get it past airport security?"

"That's easy. Just put it in your wallet."

"What about the police and their sniffer dogs?"

"Well, if you don't look dodgy, why would they hassle you and if you see the dog coming your way, go to the bathroom, get some hand soap and pop the drugs up your bum. Then rub some of the soap around you bum hole and voila, all the dog smells in hand wash."

"Wow! When you put it that way it sounds pretty easy."

"It is. Anyway, come and meet the drill and blast guys."

I introduced him around and he gets stuck talking to one of the drillers named Corey, who never shuts up about some winery he and his brother are building. He talks a lot of crap so I would not be surprised if there was no winery, and he was just making it all up.

Anyway, he is entertaining Mick who has only just started. Remember some pages back that old school friend who hit me up for a job. Well, I could not get him a job on the blast crew with me, so I got him a job doing room cleaning instead. A least now he has his foot in the door and he can try to sweet talk one of the supervisors to get him a job on the machines or something, if one comes up.

A couple of Wild Turkeys later and I see Terry run past me naked. Ha ha, this guy is the quietest guy you will ever meet at work but get some alcohol into him and his clothes come off. Ha ha. Everyone is cheering him on. I give him a clap and a cheer. He makes the night that little bit more interesting.

"Everyone, come for a swim," he yells out and heads off into the darkness towards the swimming pool.

Everyone is laughing until we hear a big bang. WTF was that? Everyone gets up and runs towards where the sound came from, and we come across Terry laying in a big hairy heap in front of the pool gate. The idiot has run headfirst into the pool gate and knocked himself out. Everyone pisses themselves laughing, the situation is so ridiculous. But after another ten seconds of him not moving we realise something is wrong and luckily Steve one of the emergency response guys is there and goes to Terry's aid. Oh well Steve has this under his control and there are plenty of people helping, I figure if I stay, I will just be in the way, so I head back to the wet mess and have a couple more Wild Turkeys, while listening to the Maori boys singing and playing their guitar. They are surprisingly good singers, a lot better than I am. I stay up to midnight and decide that is me done, back to me donga to pass out.

How did I go reader? Are you enjoying the story so far? I might take a break and you can listen to my best mate George, tell you, his story. Do not worry, I will be back to finish off the book. Bye for now.

George

Hellooo ladies and gentlemen, I am George, and this is my story of how I went from being a security guard, and a bodyguard for a drug dealer, to a FIFO worker.

Where should I start? I do not want to start with a boring story, or you will not hang around to the end. You will think, BORING... and close the book. I know! I will tell you how I started working for Sam the drug dealer.

It feels like a long time ago now, basically a different life. You know what it is like the teenage version of you is completely different to the twenty's version and so on. You think back and say to yourself, I cannot believe I was that dumb or naive, or maybe you think back and go, what a legend. I wish I was still that cool, look at me now. What the hell happened to me?

Anyway, there I was working in a nightclub in Northbridge, Western Australia. Due to my size, it is easy work. I am a naturally friendly guy and I do not like violence, that is because I grew up watching my dad use my mum as a punching bag, whenever he got drunk. I guess it is not all his fault, he grew up watching his father do the same and I am sure his father before him and so on. It is a cycle that is stopping with me. When I get married, I never want to lay a finger on my wife, and I definitely do not want my kids seeing me do it or resenting me the way I resent my dad. If you have seen the movie Once Were Warriors with Jake the Muss, that is basically how I grew up with Jake as my dad. Mum was pretty lippy to dad and when she would get drunk, she would take some swings at dad or just abuse him verbally. That was all acceptable in those days, and that is why I have no interest in Maori girls. It is whites and yellows only for me. Wow! Sorry, that probably sounded racist as, I meant Caucasians and Asians. You have to be so politically correct these days.

Back to the story, I was doing my job checking IDs and keeping an eye on the crowd for any troublemakers, that is when saw a couple of guys push another guy out towards the balcony area. I click my two-way button.

"Copy Frank."

"Yeah copy."

"Hey, I am going onto the balcony. I just saw 2 guys push another guy out there. I will let you know if I need you."

"Yep, copy that."

I walked out onto the balcony and saw one guy holding some poor bugger by the neck leaning him slightly over the railing. His mate was going through the guy's pockets.

"Oi, you two." I shout in my, I mean business tone.

"Fuck off dickhead or I'll cut you open," the pocket feeler said while flashing a knife at me.

"We will get the rest off you later," said the guy who had him by the throat. He threw him towards the ground and kicked him in the stomach.

I hate seeing people be picked on, so I grabbed the guy with the knife by the throat, twisted the knife out of his hand and threw him into the other guy knocking them both on their arses.

"You'll pay for that," said the knife guy as they both ran away.

The assaulted guy was trying to get up. He was holding his stomach, he looked winded.

"You alright bro?" I asked.

"Yeah, thanks. Thank you so much."

"No worries. Do you want me to call the police for you?"

"No, no, no it is all good, thanks."

He started quickly scooping up his things from off the ground and that is when I saw the Ecstasy pills and the little bags of speed.

"Oh, shit bro, you can't be doing that here," I said pointing to the drugs. "And no offence but you are too small for that, you are going to get jumped a lot."

"I know, this is not the first time I have been jumped for my gear."

"Well, you had better stop or get a bodyguard or something."

He looked me up and down.

"Will you be my bodyguard?"

"Ha ha, not me bro. I don't want to do anything illegal."

"You won't be. I will be. Anyway, how much do you earn here $15 or $20 an hour?"

"$22."

"Well, how's $100 sound?"

"I'm listening."

"Well, if you are interested, you can start right now. I have to sell the rest of this stuff and then if you walk me safely out of here and drive me home, that's about five hours work, so $500 cash. Easy money and you can still earn your little $22 an hour at the same time."

"Make it $150."

"$110"

"$140"

"Okay, $125. That is $625 for tonight. Tax free. You have to be happy with that."

"Sounds fair," I played it cool, but I was really thinking Wow! That is so much money for one night's work.

"Well, since you will be working for me, I had better introduce myself, I'm Sam."

"I'm George," I replied, and we shake hands.

"Well, I had better start selling this stuff. Just keep close but not too close or you might scare the customers away."

"Too easy."

The rest of the evening was uneventful. I kept doing my security work and at the same time, kept an eye on Sam. At the end of my shift, I went to find Sam, but I could not find him anywhere. That little piece of shit must have done a runner. I hate getting used. I felt myself getting angry and I wanted to put my fist through a door or through that stupid little head of his. I should have just let those guys jump him. I started thinking how stupid I was to allow myself to get used. How dumb and trusting I am. I have not told you, but I suffer from depression and once those negative voices start in my head, it is hard to turn them off. My mind starts looking for all the times I have been used or have done something stupid, to prove to myself that I am worthless and stupid. My body starts to shake and my hands close into fists and I am about to explode.

"Hey George, are you okay?"

I turn around and see Sam standing there. He looks at me and takes a couple of steps backwards. See, he did not use you, he was probably just taking a leak. I breathe in four or five big slow breathes to calm myself down. Then I smile at him to reassure him that I am fine.

"Yeah, sweet as bro. Are you ready to go?" I ask.

"Ahhh, yeah. Are you sure you are, okay?"

"Yeah, all good, bro."

I walk him out of the club and to my car. I could tell he was happy to have a bodyguard, he was walking with a bit of swagger, you know chest out, chin up like he is the man. I had to stop myself from laughing at him.

"Here we are," I say as we arrive at my car. It is a four door Toyota Corolla.

"What? This is your car? How do you fit in that?"

"I fit just fine and it's a great car, very reliable and fuel efficient. Why do you think all of the Indians buy them?"

We jump in and he gives me directions to his house.

"Come in, you can meet my Grandma."

"What? I don't think it is that official. I have not even met your parents yet and you are going straight to the grandparents. Ha ha."

"Ha ha, I think she might have some work for you too. Come and meet her."

"Umm, righto," I reply. I don't know what kind of work some grandma might have for me. We head inside.

"Hey Grandma, this is George, he is my bodyguard."

"Gee, you are a big one, aren't you? I am Judith."

"Ha ha, nice to meet you Judith," I say while gently shaking her wrinkled hand.

"I thought George might be able to help you too Grandma."

She looks at me again and then back at her grandson.

"Excuse us for a sec George. I just have to have a quick chat with my grandson."

They leave the room for a couple of minutes and when they return Judith is leading the way.

"George are you a police officer? You know you have to tell me, or it is entrapment."

"Ha ha, are you serious?"

"Please just answer the question."

"Okay, no I am not a police officer."

"Okay, would you mind taking off your shirt? So, I can check for a wire, please."

"Yeah, no worries."

I reckon she probably wants to have a perve as well; poor old duck probably has not seen a guy topless in her house for a long time.

"Please turn around."

I do the full 360.

"Good, thank you for that. You cannot be too trusting these days."

"No worries, and what kind of work would you be needing me for Judith?"

"Well for a start, when Samson needs you to keep an eye on him at the clubs, do that and we do deliveries as well, for bigger orders. So, if you can assist Samson with those, that would be helpful."

"Sounds easy enough."

"Good, well here is your $625 for tonight and Samson will give you a call in the morning, for a couple of deliveries."

I leave and cruise home. Wow! That was the easiest money I have ever made, and I still get paid for my security job on top. Winning.

Buzz, buzz. I wake up to my phone vibrating. I look down and see Sam's name on the caller ID.

"Hello," I answered.

"Hello, Bodyguard. Can you be ready in thirty minutes, and I will swing past yours?"

"Yeah, no worries," I answer and give him my address.

I was standing out the front waiting, when I see a stock standard Holden Captiva pull up.

"I thought you would be driving something a bit flasher. Like a Mercedes or BMW," I asked.

"Nope, I am smarter than that. Cops drive past this car and they think Mum or Dad taking their kid to soccer training and just keep on driving."

"Fair enough. I bet you have those stick figure family stickers on the back too, yeah?" I say while looking over the car.

"Nope, no stickers. You do not want the car to be recognisable. You want to fly under the radar as much as possible. Take a good look at me, Kmart t-shirt and shorts driving a ten-year-old Holden Captiva. No one is going to think I am transporting drugs."

"Fair enough."

I must give it to him, he has a point. This might be a good learning experience for me.

"Have you got a clean licence? No demerit points, speeding tickets, criminal record?"

"What is this, another interview? I thought I already had the job?"

"You do. I just don't want any surprises if we get pulled over."

"Na, I'm clean as."

"Great, alright you are driving, and I will tell you where to go. We have a couple of new customers."

He pulls out an old UBD. For the younger readers, this is a map book, us older people used them before we had Google Maps on our phones. Ha ha.

"God bro, that is old school. What is the address I will look it up on my phone?"

"No way. You do not want anything on your phone, that the cops can use against you later. Don't you know that is how they have convicted heaps of murderers; they go through the person's phone for where they have been. You should not even be bringing yours on this trip."

Gee, this guy is onto it. I bet he has watched all the Soprano series and every Law and Order episode. Actually, he is a bit young for that, Judith probably watched them all and told him. Ha ha, she reminds me of a female drug queen, like off that show Queen of the South or someone from that Walter White show, what was that called? It will come to me later. Oh yeah, Breaking Bad. That was a good show.

The only problem with those series, is when you need to get some sleep, but the episode finishes on a cliff hanger and you say to yourself, I will just watch the first five minutes of the next one to see what happens and before you know it, you have just watched a complete season and it is five in the morning and you have to get up for work in an hour.

Anyway, back to the story at hand. We pull up to a nice two storey house in Hillarys. There are four cars parked in the drive and you can hear music playing inside. Mind you, it is 9am in the morning, so it is either an early start for a party or the party has not stopped from the night before.

Knock, knock. No answer.

Knock, knock. Still no answer. I push Sam aside. Bang Bang.

"Shit, it is the cops," I hear someone saying from inside.

"Na, didn't you order a pizza?"

"I do remember ordering something."

"Was it Chinese?"

Knock, knock. Sam knocked again.

"You ordered party treats," Sam called through the door.

The door opened and standing there pissing themselves laughing were two hot chicks.

"Hi, sorry about that. Ha ha. I'm Sofia and this is Jackie."

"Hi, I'm Sam and this is George."

"Come in and have a drink with us."

We followed the girls into the kitchen. There were other people in the kitchen and outside by the pool. The kitchen benchtop was full of half empty bottles of spirits or half full, depending on how you look at life. Looking at all the different coloured spirits, it looked like the girls had a rather good cocktail night last night.

"Nice place, is it yours?" Sam asked Sofia.

"Na, it's an Air B n B. We do FIFO so we are only home for one week a month, so there is no point having a house. We just Air B n B a different house each time we are home."

"Fair enough. Well, I have the stuff you ordered if you have the cash."

"Yep, here you go." Sofia said while pulling out the cash.

"Umm, sorry, no offense, but I don't know these people. Can we just pop into one of the bedrooms and do the transaction without people watching."

"Wow! You are forward. Let me get this straight. Are you asking me for sex or to buy drugs. Ha ha.

Just joking, come with me," and off they go to make the transaction.

We hung around for an hour having a chat and it ends up these girls had worked with a cousin of mine up in the mines and they were trying to talk me into working up north.

"Who knows? If this security work does not work out, maybe I will," I said to them.

The other funny thing was that they told me Jackie used to be a guy, now she is a Transgender woman. God, the doctors these days can do awesome work. I could not even tell and to be honest, if they had not told me, I would probably have had a crack.

We left the girls and did a couple more deliveries, easy stuff.

"That is the last one. We will cruise back to mine and drop off the cash. Then I will drop you off home," Sam said to me as we were walking back to the car.

We get back to Sam's house and walk into the kitchen. Judith is in there cooking and right next to her in the sink, is a bag of marijuana branches. Ha ha, you do not see that every day, do you? Ha ha.

"Hey Judith, what's cooking?"

"Hi George, I am making butter and oil."

"Okay," I responded confused. "And you are using marijuana to do that?"

"Yes George, us oldies have aches and pains that you young ones do not. But do not worry, age catches up with us all and you will experience them soon enough. Enjoy your knees and back, while they are still limber."

"So, what are you telling me, is that you get stoned, so you don't have to worry about your aches and pains?"

"You do not have to get stoned or completely wasted as Samson would put it. I use the butter to make cakes and biscuits and I only eat a little bit if my arthritis is playing up. I have no aspirations of being stoned and laying on the couch all day eating pizza. As for the oil I sell it to my friends, it helps with anxiety, insomnia, epilepsy and you do not get high of it."

"Fair enough. So how do you actually make the butter and oil?"

"It is really easy. For the butter, I put 500grams of butter into the slow cooker, add some stem and leaves, fill with water and slow cook it for 24 hours. Then I use my tongs to remove the solid matter, leave it to cool. Once it has cooled, I am left with the butter on top, which I remove and freeze, the bottom half is liquid which I just tip down the sink."

"Sounds easy enough, what about the oil?"

"See that soup maker over there?"

She points to an urn; you know the type. The ones that are normally full of coffee.

"Yep."

"Well, you just put the plant into the soup maker with some oil and turn it on. I usually use coconut or grape seed oil, the thinner the better. Once it is ready, I pour it through a sift, which is a piece of material. Then I bottle and chill it."

"Very cool," I said with a newfound respect for Judith.

Judith was loving the attention. I guess the older generation are not used to the younger generation stopping and paying them our full attention.

"Have you seen how they are grown?"

"No, I haven't actually."

"Come with me."

Here we go reader, if the cooking class was not enough, you are about to get a masterclass in how to grow marijuana. Ha ha.

We walk down the hallway to a spare room, and she unlocks the door. Inside were two tall rectangular tents and a little cupboard with chemical bottles sitting on top of it.

"Would you like me to run you through the process?"

"Yes please," I said, while looking around at this crazy sight.

"Okay, well it starts here," she said as she opened the little cupboard. There were a couple of marijuana plant cuttings under a light inside. "This is the nursery. You start with a couple of clones, which are cuttings off a main plant, that you put into coconut base squares until they grow roots. Next we move one into a big pot and place it in the main tent."

She closed the cupboard and tore open the Velcro door to one of the main tents, to reveal a massive plant, it took up the whole width of the tent, again the plant had a light hanging over top of it. God the smell was strong, I could probably get high just standing here.

"You can smell that, huh? Ha ha."

"Ha ha, yep."

"I have those fans running, to bring in fresh air and take away the old smelly air. But you cannot hide it all. Anyway, that rooted clone that we put in here goes through a grow stage for 4 weeks needing the light to be on for 18 hours and off for 6 hours. Next is the bloom stage, where the light times change to 12 hours on and 12 hours off, this stage is for 7 to 8 weeks. When you see the little hairs on the buds go to about 60% brown then you cut the plant and hang it upside down to dry, turning the light off, but leaving the fans on. In a few days, the plant will be nice and dry. Then we trim it up, buds in one pile and the rest of the plant in another.

The buds are then trimmed and weighted so 28 grams of bud goes into a 3 grams sandwich bag which equals your ounce, which Sam sells for $350. And there you have it George, nothing too complicated."

For the next year, I did two nights a week security for the night club, at the same time doing bodyguard work for Sam and three days a week with Sam doing deliveries. It was good money, and I was able to upgrade my car to a F250 which is a lot more spacious than the Corolla.

It was not all fun though; I had a gun pulled on me on multiple occasions. I copped a beating when we rocked up for a delivery only to realise, we were walking into a trap and were ambushed by a group of guys waiting with weapons. Honestly, I was getting over it.

That night when I met Johnno and I had to take on five guys to get Sam's drugs and money back was the final straw. Sam was getting greedy and reckless. I had spotted on occasion, an undercover cop car following us and even driving past my house and Sam's grandma's house. I felt it was only a matter of time before we got arrested.

Here is a question for you reader, this is where the book gets interactive. Like a choose your own adventure type of book. You get to choose what happens next. Should I, do one more drug run? You know, one more big one, that will set me up for life, roll the dice, just us verses the cops, you know, where we transport a couple of million dollars' worth of drugs and walk away millionaires, but risk if we get caught going to jail. What do you say? Should I, do it? Nod your head now if you want me to do it...

Wow! Thanks for that, you obviously do not give a shit if I go to jail. Na, that was a test and you failed. Ha ha. Na, just screwing with you, that is me done; I am out. I hit my cousin up for a job in the mines and I also got Johnno a job with me too. Why? You might ask. Why care about what happens to some random bloke who I had only just met.

Well, my younger brother's name was John, and he was killed back in NZ, by some gang prospects, in some sort of initiation to become members. Apparently, they were only supposed to beat him up, but he fell in the fight and hit his head on a curb and died. So, because Johnno has the same name I kind of feel I must protect him and get him out of that life. Digging deeper, I guess you could say I was trying to save my brother by saving this guy, using him as a substitute. Some people have daddy issues, I guess I have brother issues.

Johnno and I rock up to the camp for our first day as FIFO workers and we head into the camp office.

"Hi, are you two checking in? I haven't had the pleasure," purred a curvy chick, behind the counter. I do not mind a woman with a bit of extra padding on her and her confidence is a bit of a turn on too.

Bloody Johnno started laughing his arse off at her, as she acted sexy. I bet he is into skinny chicks. He probably has a small dick, so he would be limited in positions, if he were to hook up with a larger girl. If he were to do doggy style with one, he would probably just be rubbing his little dick up against her butt cheeks. With the tip of his dick just touching the front of her vagina, like it was knocking on a set of double front doors to a house. Hello, can I come in? His dick would be saying, with the vagina replying impatiently yes, I am waiting. Ha ha, I am so funny sometimes.

"Here you go, room P12 for you, here is a map, you can find your room," she said to Johnno, but not taking her eyes off mine.

"And as for your room, it is a bit harder to find. So, I will walk you there," she said to me while licking her lips. I felt my dick swell up a bit. If she is not a massive dick tease, then it looks like game on.

"Come, follow me big boy."

I followed behind her as she strutted her stuff down the pathway in front of the dongas. I felt like a horny schoolboy following the hot teacher to the principal's office. Ha ha. It is funny the scenarios that pop into your head at times like these.

"Well, this is my room. I will just be a sec. I have to grab something."

She came back out smelling like musk and flowers. It is funny the different perfumes girls use, most of them smell like crap, but they justify it by saying "Do you know how much this cost? and it is Gucci or whatever." News flash, it is all marketing telling you it is good, and that it is worth two hundred dollars for fifteen millilitres. I am pretty sure a nice vanilla or hazelnut spray from the body shop for fifteen dollars would smell ten times better than most of that stuff.

"And here we are at your room. I'll show you where everything is," she said while looking back at me and then down to the bulge in my pants. My dick was pulsating against my rugby shorts. Which made her eyes light up. I followed her into my room, and she attacked me ripping off my shorts and, and …

Let me just say, a gentleman never tells, ha ha. I will say, it was a fantastic welcome to camp gift, which turned into a nice causal thing.

On the mining side of things, over the next two years, I learnt how to operate a dump truck, grader, excavator and a dozer. The dozer is now my main job and I love it, it is such a great machine.

Since this is a FIFO book, I had better chuck in a FIFO story. Now let me think of a good one.

There have been so many crazy things that have happened during my mining career. One guy rolled the water truck, some drillers would drill a small hole and then shit in it, due to there being a lack of toilets in the pit. The only thing wrong with that, is when one of the blast crew guys would put their tape measure down the hole to measure the depth and since it would only go down half a meter, they would think there is a rock blocking the hole and put their arm down the hole to unblock it, only to get a handful of driller's poo. Yuk. I am sure this has happened to Johnno, but he would never admit to it.

What other stories were there...? We have had a dump truck drive over a light vehicle and almost kill the guy in the driver's seat. We have had a dump truck almost go backwards over a tip head due to the material being soft and the truckie reversing too hard into the windrow. A windrow is the pile of dirt stopping you from going over the edge.

I am surprised the mines inspector has not shut the site down. It is funny though, if someone hurts themselves, they just have to sit in the crib hut on light duties for a couple of weeks instead of going home to rest. This is so the injury does not have to be reported as a lost time injury, just something minor. You FIFO workers know what I am talking about.

Okay, I know the mining story I will share with you. It ticked off one of my bucket list items. That being said, I did not know it was even on my bucket list until I did it.

Alright, here we go. It was a dark and stormy night. Na, not really. It was actually a clear and starry night. That is one of the good things, you get when you are in the middle of nowhere, you get awesome clear starry skies, with amazing sun rises and sun sets.

Back to the story. I was on the dozer pushing off the tip head, when Emma, who I was having a little thing with, calls me up on the two way and do not worry I was not doing Shirley at the same time as I was doing Emma, like I said, I am a gentleman.

"Copy dozer 1."

"Yeah, copy."

"Hey George, have you got a head lamp?"

"Yeah, why?"

"This truck apparently has an oil leak. So, I am going to pull over behind the lighting plant and check it out. Can I borrow your head lamp?"

"No worries. I will park up next to you."

Emma parks her truck up and I park my dozer next to her. We climb down and meet on the ground.

"Hello, how is your night going?" she asks.

"Yeah good. What about yours?"

"Better now. You are here."

"Ha ha, you're funny. So where is the leak?"

"What leak?"

"You said you had an oil leak."

"Oh, did I?"

"What are you playing at?"

"I'm horny."

"Ha ha, what?"

"You heard me. Let's have sex."

"Umm, alright."

I look around and the trucks are still tipping on the tip head just a hundred meters away from us. But, as we are behind the lighting plant, we can see them, but they cannot see us. So, with her up against the track of my dozer I tick that off my list. I know you were wanting details but come on, you can use your imagination. Alright take a second and think about it… Alright are you satisfied. I was, ha ha.

"Thanks for that," Emma said.

"No worries, anytime. I had better hurry up and push that tip head before the trucks double dump on me."

"Yep, and I had better drive this truck. Have fun."

"You, too."

She climbed back into the truck and drove off and I climbed back into the dozer and went about pushing off the piles of dirt left by the other trucks, who were totally unaware of what had just happened. I did find out later a couple of truckies had a good idea of what was going on. Apparently, this was not the first time someone had done something similar.

One day on break I received a frantic phone call from Johnno.

"What's up bro?" I answered.

"They stole my fucken car."

"Who stole your car?"

"Two crack whores."

"Ha ha ha ha ha ha. What? Ha ha. Sorry I should not laugh, but what the fuck?"

"I met two chicks off the internet, they got me drunk and high, and stole my car, when I could not get my dick hard."

"Ha ha. That is so crazy. So, two chicks tried to date rape you, but you could not get it up, so they stole your car instead. Are you messing with me?"

"No, I'm serious. Can you help?"

"Just call the cops."

"I can't, I'm high and they might not believe me. You did not believe me. Can you come over?"

"Alright, alright. I will be over in twenty."

"Twenty? That's ages."

"God, have a shower and clean yourself up. I am sure you probably look as good as you sound. Don't worry you have insurance. You have insurance right."

"Yes, I have insurance. The dealership made sure I had it before I drove out."

"Alright, see you soon," I hung up.

I get to Johnno's and bang on the door.

"Yo Johnno, open up."

"Glad you are here."

He told me the whole story, which was so bloody ridiculous. You could not have made up a crazier story and then we get into my car and drive around looking for his car and the girls.

Johnno's mumbling something, I think he is praying. Gee, this guy really needs to get off the drugs and clean himself up. They say you are what you around and if all he is doing to hanging out with drugged up skanks well, enough said.

I look over into a beach car park and see a new HSV commodore parked across 3 bays with the doors wide open.

"Is that your car?" I asked.

"Thank God, yep it is. They must be down the beach."

I get him to straighten up his car and we lock both our cars before heading down to the beach, to make sure the girls have not drowned in their drugged-up state.

They were not hard to find, we just had to follow their clothes down to the water, which lead us to two naked chicks splashing about in the waves.

"Oi, Johnno, come for a swim and bring your mate."

I am guessing that one is Johnno's main one. So, I bags the other one. She looks cuter anyway. Johnno and I strip off and run into the water.

"You're a big boy, aren't you?" My one says.

"Ha ha, thanks for noticing and it gets bigger."

"I'm Trace."

"I'm George, nice to meet you."

We flirt and swim around for a while and I get a cheeky hand job under the water. I love forward girls, no stuffing around, they know what they want and grab it with both hands. Ha ha. Yeah, I'm bragging. Ha ha.

"You guys want to come back to mine and chill?" Johnno asks.

"Yeah, I'm getting hungry. I might do a Macca's run first. Trace do you want to come with me?" I ask.

"Hell yeah, let's go."

We dry ourselves and head off in search of a Mac Donald's.

"Do you want to go to Johnno's or back to mine?" I ask.

"Umm, what would be more fun? Yours. Ha ha."

I text Johnno to say we are not going to his and we head back to mine. Like I said I am a gentleman, so I am not going to tell you all the naughty stuff that we got up too. But I did find out, I have a fetish or whatever you would call it. I really like lactating breasts. When I was playing with them and the milk started coming out, she let me suck on them and it got her aroused having a grown man doing it. Which in turn, turned me on even more. And we will leave it at that. Ha ha.

Fast forward four years and…

"Hey George, do you and Trace want to come to Thailand this break?" Johnno asked.

"Maybe, who's going?"

"Me and Charlene, and Tim said he is going, but he will be doing his own thing."

"Yeah, sounds good. I will ask Trace but shouldn't be a problem."

Johnno

Hey reader, it is me, Johnno. Back to finish off the book. Did you miss me? Hopefully, George did not bore you too much. I thought I would tell you this story, as I tell it better.

We arrive at the Ramada Resort, Thailand. It is awesome, frangipani trees everywhere, our room overlooks one of the five pools, and every pool has a swim up bar. I organised there to be rose petals on the bed, in a shape of a love heart and rose petals leading up to the bed.

"Oh my god, Johnno you are so romantic. Thank you. You're amazing," Charlene said before hugging me and sticking her tongue halfway down my throat.

"Do you want to have a spa together?" She asked.

Yeah, you know it. I went the spa suite. Why not? With the Aussie dollar being so good compared to the Thai Baht lets live it up.

Anyway, this holiday is going to be one that she will never forget. Spoiler alert, yep, I am going to ask her to marry me. That is only if I can find where I packed the ring and I better find it, as it cost me a fortune, it is from Michael Hills, not a cheapy from Prouds. Not that Charlene would have cared either way. She is pretty low maintenance, which is nice for a change.

I run us a spa bath and we relax in there for a while. Just to think, this is what it is going to be like for the rest of our lives, just the two us, well until kids come along anyway. But you know what I mean.

We hop out, dry off and cuddle up for a bit, on the bed and you know what cuddling leads too. That's right, sex and then a nap. Ha ha.

Bang, bang, bang.

WTF? Oh, the door. God, I was out to it. I was dreaming I was back at work in the magazine. The magazine is what we call the sea container that contains all the explosives that we use on the blast crew. The dumb thing was, I had left the Bomb Ute back on the blast pattern and now I would have to carry all the explosives by hand back to the pattern. Which was located three kilometres away. It is funny how things like that, would not make sense in real life but in a dream, they do, they are just annoying, and you are like, damn it, how did I forget to bring the Ute, not thinking how would I have even got to the magazine without actually having driven there in the first place. Crazy stuff the old dreams.

Bang, bang, bang.

"Are you going to get that, or do you want me too?" Charlene asked.

"I will get it. It's just George."

I could tell by his knock or should I say bang. Whenever he does it, I feel like the door is about to come off its hinges. I am surprised how they don't. Anyway, I grab one of the hotel's fluffy white robes and pop it on before opening the door.

"What's up George?"

"Nothing. What's up with you? Na, you guys want to come to dinner with us?"

"Yep, gee time got away from us. Give us twenty and we will swing past yours."

"Na, we are already ready. Meet us at the View. That's the hotel's main bar."

"Okay, see you soon."

We got ready and headed down through the manicured gardens and past the pools. We walk past a family who were talking.

"That man must have drunk too much alcohol," a little girl was saying to her dad.

"Yep, some people just don't know when to stop," he replied.

Ha ha, they must have walked past some drunk Aussie throwing his guts up.

"Hey bro," George greeted us.

"Hey, what do you guys feeling like eating?" I asked.

"Pizza," replied Trace.

"Babe, we are in Thailand. Don't you want to try the local food?" George asked.

"Yeah, whatever. I was just giving my answer. We were asked a question and I can give my opinion," Trace said while glaring at George.

Whoa, must be that time of the month.

"I'm easy, whatever," Charlene added.

"I'm pretty sure we can find a restaurant that has both pizza and Thai food."

I ask the barman and he suggests one of the hotel's restaurants called Dream. We head over to it, and it is very flash, and would you have guessed it? On the menu is both pizza and Thai food.

We ate up and it all tasted pretty good.

"What is everyone up for? Do you want to go and watch some Muay Thai?" I asked.

"Yeah, I wouldn't mind seeing someone get their head smashed in," answered Trace.

Ha ha, such a classy chick. Everyone was happy with the Muay Thai idea. So, we pay the bill and walk the ten minutes down the road to the Muay Thai arena.

Thud, thud, bang, bang. God, these guys are going hard. I would not like to be jumping into the ring with one of those guys. We order some drinks and settle down to watch the fights.

"Hello everyone, we need a volunteer, from the crowd to fight one of our fighters," the announcer called out to the crowd.

"Go on George," Trace says.

"What? And hurt that little guy, he cannot be much older than fifteen," George answered.

Before Trace could respond.

"Hey, over here," it was Tim yelling out.

"Hey, looks like Tim is going to do it," I say.

"Nope it's Mick, see."

I look at Mick and then at Tim. Tim has a look on his face, like he had just set Mick up.

"Ha ha, look at Tim's face. This is a set up."

"Yep, for sure. Tim knows Mick won't stand a chance."

"Go Mick," we yell out and the rest of the crowd were cheering him on too. He did a fist pump to the crowd as he entered the ring. We order another round of drinks.

"Fight," the announcer called out.

Pow, bang, bang, thud and Mick was on his arse.

"Oh shit, that guy made him piss," Trace said before downing her forth Mai Tai in one massive gulp. Did I just see that? I think she just literally poured that straight down her throat with swallowing mouthfuls, just straight down. Wow! Lucky George. The way she is downing these drinks, she will be the next one on her arse. Ha ha.

"He is back up. Go Mick, smash him," George yelled out. The crowd cheered for Mick again.

Pow, bang, bang, thud. Oh shit, that was a bit rough. The guy finished him with a kick to the head and Mick was out for the count.

"Should we go down there and see if he is alright?" I ask.

"Give him a minute. Tim is down there with him."

Twenty seconds later, Mick stands up.

"He is all good," the announcer called to the crowd.

The crowd cheered as Tim helped Mick back to the stands.

"You guys want to cruise?" George asks.

"Yeah, let's go clubbing. This is boring as shit. I thought there was going to be blood everywhere. These guys are soft. I have had fights way bloodier than these," Trace slurs.

I look at Charlene.

"Ha ha, don't worry Johnno. I have seen her in worse shape. She'll be right. Yeah, let's go clubbing," Charlene reassured me.

We leave the arena and bump into Tim and Mick getting into a Tuk Tuk.

"Hey Mick, good on you for giving it a go," I say.

"Thanks, Tim tricked me into it."

"At least you will have a good story to tell Sofia."

"That's what I said," Tim agreed.

"What? Am I the only one that doesn't realise Sofia likes me?"

"Well, I don't," Trace piped in and finished that comment with a massive burp.

"Ha ha. Yeah, well everyone at work knows. It is pretty obvious."

"You guys want to come clubbing?" George asked.

"Ha ha. Na, I had better let our Muay Thai fighter here get some rest. Who knows, he might even have a concussion or something? You guys have fun."

"You too."

With that, they hopped into their Tuk Tuk and zoomed off down the street and we walked towards the nightclubs.

It was a good night of dancing and drinking, until Trace got us kicked out.

"All I was asking, is if the ladyboys have bigger or smaller dicks than normal guys. It makes sense, doesn't it? Their bodies are turning into a woman's body. So, they don't need a big dick."

Trace was trying to justify herself, after offending a large group of ladyboys that were at the last club. Just then Trace commenced operation throw up on everyone in range. It was the power spew to end all power spews and she did not put her head down to do it. She wanted to look up and turn around while she was doing it. We all jumped back as quickly as we could to avoid being covered in it. Thanks Trace, we all ended up wearing some of her vomit, either on our shoes or clothes.

"Time to call it a night," George announced.

"Copy that," I replied.

The next morning, I snuck out of the room around 9amish, leaving Charlene snoring away in our bed.

She only snores when she has been drinking. I must say she can handle her alcohol a lot better than Trace. I hope for George's sake she just passed out when they got back to their room. There is nothing worse than a drunk girlfriend wanting to have a deep and meaningful conversation all night long and the stupid thing is, when they don't even remember any of it the next day, and you had spent hours of your night tortured for no reason.

Anyway, I was on a mission. I went to the front desk and told them what I wanted to do, and they sat me down with an events / tour guide person and we worked it all out.

After all that was sorted, I went to the breakfast buffet, to get some breakfast to take back for Charlene.

"Oh hello," I say, surprised. George, Trace and Charlene were all sitting down for breakfast.

"Where did you sneak off too?" Charlene asked.

"The gym," I replied, thinking quickly.

"Ha ha," George laughed, "you haven't been to the gym in the whole time that I have known you and you are wearing thongs."

Wow! Great friend he is. You would think he would know when to shut up. I gave him a look to say, "Shut up. You are ruining everything."

"You're being dodgy Johnno. Are you hooking up with some other bird or a ladyboy from last night?" Charlene asked, half joking.

"No, fuck no."

"Hmm, well. You are full of shit about the gym. So where were you really?"

"It was supposed to be a surprise, but you all ruined it. I booked us on an elephant tour today.

We leave in an hour and George; you owe me $100 bucks for it."

"Wow! Thanks for spending my money without asking."

"You will thank me. It'll be fun."

"Hmm, is that really it? You still have a dodgy vibe going on."

"Wow! A guy tries to do something nice, and he gets attitude."

"Whatever. Have some breakfast, the juices are fresh as. A bit of vitamin C always helps after a big night."

We finish up breakfast and get ready.

"This is our ride," I say pointing to the driver and his minivan. We all hop in and drive to the elephant park place.

We arrive and each couple are given an elephant to ride on and a guide who walks next to the elephant, leading it along the path and through a stream. It is very pretty; we are going through the jungle and because the vegetation is so thick, it feels like we are the only ones there. Very peaceful.

"You can sit on the elephant's shoulders, just behind its head if you want," the guide said to me. So, I shuffled forward onto the elephant's shoulders and placed my legs either side of the elephant's head just behind its ears. They are quite hairy when you are up this close. This was really cool. You feel like a real jungle guy riding an elephant like this, ha ha.

We finish the ride and are treated to a nice lunch in a wooden hut in the jungle with fresh fruit as desert. We hop back into the minivan and cruise back to the hotel, where we spend the rest of the day relaxing by the pool. At night, the locals are selling those paper lantern things that you write yours and your girlfriend's names on, within a love heart. Then they light a candle that is attached to it, and the lantern thing floats up into the sky and flies away out of view, very romantic. Something that you would see in a Rom Com, a Romantic Comedy.

The next day, we are going snorkelling and hop back into our minivan and are driven to a boat ramp.

"I haven't been snorkelling since I was in high school," Charlene said.

"Yeah, I remember that. It was in Outdoor Education with Mr Sleazy. What was his real name? He would always try to sneak a peek up the girl's skirts or down their tops," Trace said.

"Mr Adams."

"Yeah, that's right, Mr Adams. I'm pretty sure, he got arrested for setting up a camera in the girl's toilets."

"That would not surprise me."

We hop onto the boat and cruise past the islands and the tall rocky island things that stick up out of the water in the middle of the ocean. Eventually the boat pulls up at our island. We are given a snorkel set with flippers and we go snorkelling. I must say there is not much coral here, not compared to Australia. I have been to Coral Bay and that is a million times better than this. It is still fun swimming around and watching Charlene in her skimpy little bikini and the fact that she had no idea what is about to come next is pretty awesome.

We swim around for another twenty minutes or so and then dry off and relax on our towels.

"Mr Peterson?" a local guy asks me.

"Yep, that is me. You can call me John if you want."

"Okay John, would your group like to follow me please?"

"Where are we going?" Charlene asked.

"You will see."

The four of us follow the guide down a sandy path to a more secluded part of the beach. My guts were twisting and turning, and I was feeling sick.

We arrive at the secluded beach I was promised and there are rose petals making a path to a picnic blanket with more rose petals on top and a basket with some beers and a fruit platter. I went for beers instead of champagne because it tastes better. We have never been big champagne people and if I did it, it would have just been to follow the pack as everyone does that and I am not a sheep.

"Come with me," I say to Charlene.

I take her by the hand and lead her over to the blanket. I get down on one knee and pull out the ring.

"Charlene, will you marry me?" I feel sick and I almost throw up in my mouth. You know those little in your mouth spews, that you have to swallow, and it tastes gross.

"Yes, yes of course I will," she was so happy. Thank God, it would have gotten really awkward, if she had said no. We hug and have a big pash. George, Trace and the guide were all clapping and wolf whistling.

"Oh my god. I was so nervous," I say.

"Ha ha, so that was why you were acting so dodgy. I knew something was up."

"Ha ha, yeah. I don't have the best poker face."

Boom! Well, there you have it. How was that reader? I told you it was going to be a bit of a wide ride. We had a grandma with a hydro setup, a bikie's daughter hooking up with the main character, a stolen car, a breast feeding single mother, a drug dealer getting bashed in the toilets, a marriage proposal and it was all perfectly intertwined with the first FIFO novel. See how you even met Sofia and Jackie randomly.

Thanks for reading the book and same as with the first book, feel free to reach out to the author on social media and tell him what you honestly thought of the book and tell a friend or a work mate about the book. The more people that know about it the better. Thanks again and we will see you next time in FIFO 3.

About the Author

Aron started his mining career as a driller's offsider, on an RC drill rig, back in 2003. Then he landed a job doing FIFO, as a blast crew labourer and earnt his shot firers licence. When he realised a dump truck operator got paid the same as a shotfirer, he made the transition into the air conditioning and has been operating the big mining machines ever since.

He has self-published eight children's books and has a podcast called The Aaron White Show and is currently writing a series of these FIFO novels.

www.ingramcontent.com/pod-product-compliance
Lightning Source LLC
Chambersburg PA
CBHW070615120726
47909CB00004B/1229